A Case of the Claws

A Case of the Claws

Ellis Peters • Patricia Highsmith
Catherine Aird • Edmund Crispin

Profile Books

First published in Great Britain in 2025 by
Profile Books Ltd
29 Cloth Fair
London
EC1A 7JQ

www.profilebooks.com

See page 90 for individual stories' copyright information
Illustrations © Joanna Lisowiec

SRD

Typeset in Freight Text by MacGuru Ltd

Printed and bound in India by
Manipal Technologies Limited, Manipal

The moral right of the author has been asserted.

A CIP catalogue record for this book is available from the British
Library.

Our product safety representative in the EU is Authorised Rep
Compliance Ltd., Ground Floor, 71 Lower Baggot Street, Dublin,
D02 P593, Ireland. www.arccompliance.com

ISBN 978 1 80522 6086
eISBN 978 1 80522 6093

Contents

Contents

The Trinity Cat

Ellis Peters

HE WAS SITTING ON TOP of one of the rear gateposts of the churchyard when I walked through on Christmas Eve, grooming in his lordly style, with one back leg wrapped round his neck, and his bitten ear at an angle of forty-five degrees, as usual. I reckon one of the toms he'd tangled with in his nomad days had ripped the starched bit out of that one, the other stood up sharply enough. There was snow on the ground, a thin veiling, just beginning to crackle in promise of frost before evening, but he had at least three warm refuges around the place whenever he felt like holing up, besides his two houses, which he used only for visiting and cadging.

He'd been a known character around our village for three years then, ever since he walked in from nowhere and made himself agreeable to the vicar and the verger, and finding the billet comfortable and the pickings good, constituted himself resident cat to Holy Trinity Church, and took over all the jobs around the place that humans were too slow to tackle, like rat-catching, and chasing off invading dogs.

Nobody knows how old he is, but I think he could only have been about two when he settled here, a scrawny, chewed-up black bandit as lean as wire. After three years of being fed by Joel Woodward at Trinity Cottage, which was the verger's house by tradition, and flanked the lych-gate on one side, and pampered and petted by Miss Patience Thomson at Church Cottage on the other side, he was double his old size, and sleek as velvet, but still had one lop ear and a kink two inches from the end of his tail. He still looked like a brigand, but a highly prosperous brigand. Nobody ever gave him a name, he wasn't the sort to get called anything fluffy or familiar. Only Miss Patience ever dared coo at him, and he was very gracious about that, she being elderly and innocent and very free with little perks like raw liver, on which he doted. One way and another, he had it made. He lived mostly outdoors, never staying in either house overnight. In winter he had his own little ground-level hatch into the furnace room of the church, sharing his lodgings matily with a hedgehog that had qualified as assistant vermin-destructor around the churchyard, and preferred sitting out the winter among the coke to hibernating like common hedgehogs. These individualists keep turning up in our valley, for some reason.

All I'd gone to the church for that afternoon was to fix up with the vicar about the Christmas peal, having been roped into the bell-ringing team. Resident police in remote areas like ours get dragged into all sorts of activities, and when the area's changing, and new problems cropping up, if they have any sense they don't need too much dragging, but go willingly. I've put my finger on many an astonished yobbo who thought he'd got clean away with his little breaking-and-entering, just by keeping my ears open during a darts match, or choir practice.

When I came back through the churchyard, around half past two, Miss Patience was just coming out of her gate, with a shopping bag on her wrist, and heading towards the street, and we walked along together a bit of the way. She was getting on for seventy, and hardly bigger than a bird, but very independent. Never having married or left the valley, and having looked after a mother who lived to be nearly ninety, she'd never had time to catch up with new ideas in the style of dress suitable for elderly ladies. Everything had always been done mother's way, and fashion, music and morals had stuck at the period when mother was a carefully brought-up girl learning domestic skills, and preparing for a chaste marriage.

There's a lot to be said for it! But it had turned Miss Patience into a frail little lady in long-skirted black or grey or navy blue, who still felt undressed without hat and gloves, at an age when Mrs Newcombe, for instance, up at the pub, favoured shocking pink trouser suits and red-gold hairpieces. A pretty little old lady Miss Patience was, though, very straight and neat. It was a pleasure to watch her walk. Which is more than I could say for Mrs Newcombe in her trouser suit, especially from the back!

'A happy Christmas, Sergeant Moon!' she chirped at me on sight. And I wished her the same, and slowed up to her pace.

'It's going to be slippery by twilight,' I said. 'You be careful how you go.'

'Oh, I'm only going to be an hour or so,' she said serenely. 'I shall be home long before the frost sets in. I'm only doing the last bit of Christmas shopping. There's a cardigan I have to collect for Mrs Downs.' That was her cleaning lady, who went in three mornings a week. 'I ordered it long ago, but deliveries are so slow nowadays. They've promised it for today. And a gramophone record for my little errand boy.' Tommy Fowler that was, one of the church trebles, as pink and wholesome-looking as they usually contrive to be, and just as artful. 'And one mustn't forget our dumb friends, either, must one?' said Miss Patience cheerfully. 'They're all important, too.'

I took this to mean a couple of packets of some new product to lure wild birds to her garden. The Church Cottage thrushes were so fat they could hardly fly, and when it was frosty she put out fresh water three or four times a day.

We came to our brief street of shops, and off she went, with her big jet-and-gold brooch gleaming in her scarf. She had quite a few pieces of Victorian and Edwardian jewellery her mother'd left behind, and almost always wore one piece, being used to the belief that a lady dresses meticulously every day, not just on Sundays. And I went for a brisk walk round to see what was going on, and then went home to Molly and high tea, and took my boots off thankfully.

That was Christmas Eve. Christmas Day little Miss Thomson didn't turn up for eight o'clock Communion, which was unheard of. The vicar said he'd call in after matins and see that she was all right, and hadn't taken cold trotting about in the snow. But somebody else beat us both to it. Tommy Fowler! He was anxious about that pop record of his. But even he had no chance until after service, for in our village it's the custom for the choir to go and sing the vicar an aubade in the shape of 'Christians, Awake!' before the main service, ignoring the fact that he's then been up four hours, and conducted two Communions. And Tommy Fowler had a solo in the anthem, too. It was a quarter past twelve when he got away, and shot up the garden path to the door of Church Cottage.

He shot back even faster a minute later. I was heading for home when he came rocketing out of the gate and ran slam into me, with his eyes sticking out on stalks and his mouth wide open, making a sort of muted keening sound with shock. He clutched hold of me and pointed back towards Miss Thomson's front door, left half-open when he fled, and tried three times before he could croak out:

'Miss Patience ... She's there on the floor – she's bad!'

I went in on the run, thinking she'd had a heart attack all alone there, and was lying helpless. The front door led through a diminutive hall, and through another glazed door into the living room, and that

door was open, too, and there was Miss
Patience face down on the carpet, still in
her coat and gloves, and with her shopping
bag lying beside her. An occasional table
had been knocked over in her fall, spilling
a vase and a book. Her hat was askew over
one ear, and caved in like a trodden mush-
room, and her neat grey bun of hair had
come undone and trailed on her shoulder,
and it was no longer grey but soiled, brown-
ish black. She was dead and stiff. The room
was so cold, you could tell those doors had
been ajar all night.

The kid had followed me in, hanging on
to my sleeve, his teeth chattering. 'I didn't
open the door – it was open! I didn't touch
her, or anything. I only came to see if she
was all right, and get my record.'

It was there, lying unbroken, half out of
the shopping bag by her arm. She'd meant
it for him, and I told him he should have it,
but not yet, because it might be evidence,
and we mustn't move anything. And I got
him out of there quick, and gave him to the
vicar to cope with, and went back to Miss

Patience as soon as I'd telephoned for the outfit. Because we had a murder on our hands.

So that was the end of one gentle, harmless old woman, one of very many these days, battered to death because she walked in on an intruder who panicked. Walked in on him, I judged, not much more than an hour after I left her in the street. Everything about her looked the same as then, the shopping bag, the coat, the hat, the gloves. The only difference, that she was dead. No, one more thing! No handbag, unless it was under the body, and later, when we were able to move her, I wasn't surprised to see that it wasn't there. Handbags are where old ladies carry their money. The sneak thief who panicked and lashed out at her had still had greed and presence of mind enough to grab the bag as he fled. Nobody'd have to describe that bag to me, I knew it well, soft black leather with an old-fashioned gilt clasp and a short handle, a small thing, not like the holdalls they carry nowadays.

She was lying facing the opposite door,

also open, which led to the stairs. On the writing desk by that door stood one of a pair of heavy brass candlesticks. Its fellow was on the floor beside Miss Thomson's body, and though the bun of hair and the felt hat had prevented any great spattering of blood, there was blood enough on the square base to label the weapon. Whoever had hit her had been just sneaking down the stairs, ready to leave. She'd come home barely five minutes too soon.

Upstairs, in her bedroom, her bits of jewellery hadn't taken much finding. She'd never thought of herself as having valuables, or of other people as coveting them. Her gold and turquoise and funereal jet and true-lover's-knots in gold and opals, and mother's engagement and wedding rings, and her little Edwardian pendant watch set with seed pearls, had simply lived in the small top drawer of her dressing table. She belonged to an honest epoch, and it was gone, and now she was gone after it. She didn't even lock her door when she went shopping. There wouldn't have been so much as the warning of a key grating in the lock, just the door opening.

Ten years ago not a soul in this valley behaved differently from Miss Patience. Nobody locked doors, sometimes not even overnight. Some of us went on a fortnight's holiday and left the doors unlocked. Now we can't even put out the milk money until the milkman knocks at the door in person. If this generation likes to pride itself on its progress, let it! As for me, I thought suddenly that maybe the innocent was well out of it.

We did the usual things, photographed the body and the scene of the crime, the doctor examined her and authorised her removal, and confirmed what I'd supposed about the approximate time of her death. And the forensic boys lifted a lot of smudgy latents that weren't going to be of any use to anybody, because they weren't going to be on record, barring a million-to-one chance. The whole thing stank of the amateur. There wouldn't be any easy matching up of prints, even if they got beauties. One more thing we did for Miss Patience. We tolled the dead bell for her on Christmas night, six heavy, muffled strokes. She was a virgin. Nobody had to vouch for it, we all knew. And let me point out, it is a title of honour, to be respected accordingly.

We'd hardly got the poor soul out of the house when the Trinity cat strolled in, taking advantage of the minute or two while the door was open. He got as far as the place on the carpet where she'd lain, and his fur and whiskers stood on end, and even his lop ear jerked up straight. He put his nose down to the pile of the Wilton, about where her shopping bag and handbag must have lain, and started going round in interested circles, snuffing the floor and making little throaty noises that might have been distress, but sounded like pleasure. Excitement, anyhow. The chaps from the CID were still busy, and didn't want him under their feet, so I picked him up and took him with me when I went across to Trinity Cottage to talk to the verger.

The cat never liked being picked up, after

a minute he started clawing and cursing, and I put him down. He stalked away again at once, past the corner where people shot their dead flowers, out at the lych-gate, and straight back to sit on Miss Thomson's doorstep. Well, after all, he used to get fed there, he might well be uneasy at all these queer comings and goings. And they don't say 'as curious as a cat' for nothing, either.

I didn't need telling that Joel Woodward had had no hand in what had happened, he'd been nearest neighbour and good friend to Miss Patience for years, but he might have seen or heard something out of the ordinary. He was a little, wiry fellow, gnarled like a tree root, the kind that goes on spry and active into his nineties, and then decides that's enough, and leaves overnight. His wife was dead long ago, and his daughter had come back to keep house for him after her husband deserted her, until she died, too, in a bus accident. There was just old Joel now, and the grandson she'd left with him, young Joel Barnett, nineteen, and a bit of a tearaway by his grandad's standards, but so far pretty innocuous by mine. He was a sulky, graceless sort, but he did work, and he stuck with the old man when many another would have lit out elsewhere.

'A bad business,' said old Joel, shaking his head. 'I only wish I could help you lay hands on whoever did it. But I only saw her yesterday morning about ten, when she took in the milk. I was round at the church hall all afternoon, getting things ready for the youth social they had last night, it was dark before I got back. I never saw or heard anything out of place. You can't see her living-room light from here, so there was no call to wonder. But the lad was here all afternoon. They only work till one, Christmas Eve. Then they all went boozing together for an hour or so, I expect, so I don't know exactly what time he got in, but he was here and had the tea on when I came home. Drop round in an hour or so and he should be here, he's gone round to collect this girl he's mashing. There's a party somewhere tonight.'

I dropped round accordingly, and young Joel was there, sure enough, shoulder-length hair, frilled shirt, outsize lapels and all, got up to kill, all for the benefit of the girl his grandad had mentioned. And it turned out to be Connie Dymond, from the comparatively respectable branch of the family, along the canal-side. There were three sets of Dymond cousins, boys, no great harm in 'em but worth watching, but only this one girl in Connie's family. A good-looker, or at least most of the lads seemed to think so, she had a dozen or so on her string before she took up with young Joel. Big girl, too, with a lot of mauve eyeshadow and a mother-of-pearl mouth, in huge platform shoes and the fashionable drab granny-coat. But she was acting very prim and proper with old Joel around.

'Half past two when I got home,' said young Joel. 'Grandad was round at the hall, and I'd have gone round to help him, only I'd had a pint or two, and after I'd had me dinner I went to sleep, so it wasn't worth it by the time I woke up. Around four, that'd be. From then on I was here watching the telly, and I never saw nor heard a thing. But there was nobody else here, so I could be spinning you the yarn, if you want to look at it that way.'

He had a way of going looking for trouble before anybody else suggested it, there was nothing new about that. Still, there it was. One young fellow on the spot, and minus any alibi. There'd be plenty of others in the same case.

In the evening he'd been at the church social. Miss Patience wouldn't be expected there, it was mainly for the young, and anyhow, she very seldom went out in the evenings.

'I was there with Joel,' said Connie Dymond. 'He called for me at seven, I was with him all the evening. We went home to our place after the social finished, and he didn't leave till nearly midnight.'

Very firm about it she was, doing her best for him. She could hardly know that his movements in the evening didn't interest us, since Miss Patience had then been dead for some hours.

When I opened the door to leave the

Trinity cat walked in, stalking past me with a purposeful stride. He had a look round us all, and then made for the girl, reached up his front paws to her knees, and was on her lap before she could fend him off, though she didn't look as if she welcomed his attentions. Very civil he was, purring and rubbing himself against her coat sleeve, and poking his whiskery face into hers. Unusual for him to be effusive, but when he did decide on it, it was always with someone who couldn't stand cats. You'll have noticed it's a way they have.

'Shove him off,' said young Joel, seeing she didn't at all care for being singled out. 'He only does it to annoy people.'

And she did, but he only jumped on again, I noticed as I closed the door on them and left. It was a Dymond party they were going to, the senior lot, up at the filling station. Not much point in trying to check up on all her cousins and swains when they were gathered for a booze-up. Coming out of a hangover, tomorrow, they might be easy meat. Not that I had any special reason to look their way, they were an extrovert lot, more given to grievous bodily harm in street punch-ups than anything secretive. But it was wide open.

Well, we summed up. None of the lifted prints was on record, all we could do in that line was exclude all those that were Miss Thomson's. This kind of sordid little opportunist break-in had come into local experience only fairly recently, and though it was no novelty now, it had never before led to a death. No motive but the impulse of greed, so no traces leading up to the act, and none leading away. Everyone connected with the church, and most of the village besides, knew about the bits of jewellery she had, but never before had anyone considered them as desirable loot. Victoriana now carry inflated values, and are in demand, but this still didn't look calculated, just wanton. A kid's crime, a teenager's crime. Or the crime of a permanent teenager. They start at twelve years old now, but there are also the shiftless louts who never get beyond twelve years old, even in their forties.

We checked all the obvious people: her part-time gardener – but he was demonstrably elsewhere at the time – and his drifter of a son, whose alibi was non-existent but voluble; the window cleaner, a sidelong soul who played up his ailments and did rather well out of her; all the delivery men. Several there who were clear, one or two who could have been around, but had no particular reason to be.

Then we went after all the youngsters who, on their records, were possibles. There were three with breaking-and-entering convictions, but if they'd been there they'd been gloved. Several others with petty theft against them were also without alibis. By the end of a pretty exhaustive survey the field was wide, and none of the runners seemed to be ahead of the rest, and we were still looking. None of the stolen property had so far showed up.

Not, that is, until the Saturday. I was coming from Church Cottage through the graveyard again, and as I came near the corner where the dead flowers were shot,

I noticed a glaring black patch making an irregular hole in the veil of frozen snow that still covered the ground. You couldn't miss it, it showed up like a black eye. And part of it was the soil and rotting leaves showing through, and part, the blackest part, was the Trinity cat, head down and back arched, digging industriously like a terrier after a rat. The bent end of his tail lashed steadily, while the remaining eight inches stood erect.

If he knew I was standing watching him, he didn't care. Nothing was going to deflect him from what he was doing. And in a minute or two he heaved his prize clear, and clawed out to the light a little black leather handbag with a gilt clasp. No mistaking it, all stuck over as it was with dirt and rotting leaves. And he loved it, he was patting it and playing with it and rubbing his head against it, and purring like a steam engine. He cursed, though, when I took it off him, and walked round and round me, pawing and swearing, telling me and the world he'd found it, and it was his.

It hadn't been there long. I'd been along that path often enough to know that the snow hadn't been disturbed the day before. Also, the mess of humus fell off it pretty quick and clean, and left it hardly stained at all. I held it in my handkerchief and snapped the catch, and the inside was clean and empty, the lining slightly frayed from long use. The Trinity cat stood upright on his hind legs and protested loudly, and he had a voice that could outshout a Siamese.

Somebody behind me said curiously: 'Whatever've you got there?' And there was young Joel standing open-mouthed, staring, with Connie Dymond hanging on to his arm and gaping at the cat's find in horrified recognition.

'Oh, no! My gawd, that's Miss Thomson's bag, isn't it? I've seen her carrying it hundreds of times.'

'Did *he* dig it up?' said Joel, incredulous. 'You reckon the chap who – you know, *him*! – he buried it there? It could be anybody, everybody uses this way through.'

'My gawd!' said Connie, shrinking in

fascinated horror against his side. 'Look at that cat! You'd think he *knows* ... He gives me the shivers! What's got into him?'

What, indeed? After I'd got rid of them and taken the bag away with me I was still wondering. I walked away with his prize and he followed me as far as the road, howling and swearing, and once I put the bag down, open, to see what he'd do, and he pounced on it and started his fun and games again until I took it from him. For the life of me I couldn't see what there was about it to delight him, but he was in no doubt. I was beginning to feel right superstitious about this avenging detective cat, and to wonder what he was going to unearth next.

I know I ought to have delivered the bag to the forensic lab, but somehow I hung on to it overnight. There was something fermenting at the back of my mind that I couldn't yet grasp.

Next morning we had two more at morning service besides the regulars. Young Joel hardly ever went to church, and I doubt if anybody'd ever seen Connie

Dymond there before, but there they both were, large as life and solemn as death, in a middle pew, the boy sulky and scowling as if he'd been press-ganged into it, as he certainly had, Connie very subdued and big-eyed, with almost no make-up and an unusually grave and thoughtful face. Sudden death brings people up against daunting possibilities, and creates penitents. Young Joel felt silly there, but he was daft about her, plainly enough, she could get him to do what she wanted, and she'd wanted to make this gesture. She went through all the movements of devotion, he just sat, stood and kneeled awkwardly as required, and went on scowling.

There was a bitter east wind when we came out. On the steps of the porch everybody dug out gloves and turned up collars against it, and so did young Joel, and as he hauled his gloves out of his coat pocket, out with them came a little bright thing that rolled down the steps in front of us all and came to rest in a crack between the flagstones of the path. A gleam of pale blue and gold. A dozen people must have recognised it. Mrs Downs gave tongue in a shriek that informed even those who hadn't.

'That's Miss Thomson's! It's one of her turquoise earrings! *How did you get hold of that, Joel Barnett?*'

How, indeed? Everybody stood staring at the tiny thing, and then at young Joel, and he was gazing at the flagstones, struck white and dumb. And all in a moment Connie Dymond had pulled her arm free of his and recoiled from him until her back was against the wall, and was edging away from him like somebody trying to get out of range of flood or fire, and her face a sight to be seen, blind and stiff with horror.

'You!' she said in a whisper. 'It was you! Oh, my God, *you* did it – *you* killed her! And me keeping company – how could I? How could *you*!'

She let out a screech and burst into sobs, and before anybody could stop her she turned and took to her heels, running for home like a mad thing.

I let her go. She'd keep. And I got young

Joel and that single earring away from the Sunday congregation and into Trinity Cottage before half the people there knew what was happening, and shut the world out, all but old Joel who came panting and shaking after us a few minutes later.

The boy was a long time getting his voice back, and when he did he had nothing to say but, hopelessly, over and over: 'I didn't! I never touched her, I wouldn't. I don't know how that thing got into my pocket. I didn't do it. I never ...'

Human beings are not all that inventive. Given a similar set of circumstances they tend to come out with the same formula. And in any case, 'deny everything and say nothing else' is a very good rule when cornered.

They thought I'd gone round the bend when I said: 'Where's the cat? See if you can get him in.'

Old Joel was past wondering. He went out and rattled a saucer on the steps, and pretty soon the Trinity cat strolled in. Not at all excited, not wanting anything, fed and lazy, just curious enough to come and see why he was wanted. I turned him loose on young Joel's overcoat, and he couldn't have cared less. The pocket that had held the earring held very little interest for him. He didn't care about any of the clothes in the wardrobe, or on the pegs in the little hall. As far as he was concerned, this new find was a non-event.

I sent for a constable and a car, and took young Joel in with me to the station, and all the village, you may be sure, either saw us pass or heard about it very shortly after. But I didn't stop to take any statement from him, just left him there, and took the car up to Mary Melton's place, where she breeds Siamese, and borrowed a cat basket from her, the sort she uses to carry her queens to the vet. She asked what on earth I wanted it for, and I said to take the Trinity cat for a ride. She laughed her head off.

'Well, *he's* no queen,' she said, 'and no king, either. Not even a jack! And you'll never get that wild thing into a basket.'

'Oh, yes, I will,' I said. 'And if he isn't any

of the other picture cards, he's probably going to turn out to be the joker.'

A very neat basket it was, not too obviously meant for a cat. And it was no trick getting the Trinity cat into it; all I did was drop in Miss Thomson's handbag, and he was in after it in a moment. He growled when he found himself shut in, but it was too late to complain then.

At the house by the canal Connie Dymond's mother let me in, but was none too happy about letting me see Connie, until I explained that I needed a statement from her before I could fit together young Joel's movements all through those Christmas days.

Naturally I understood that the girl was terribly upset, but she'd had a lucky escape, and the sooner everything was cleared up, the better for her. And it wouldn't take long.

It didn't take long. Connie came down the stairs readily enough when her mother called her. She was all stained and pale and tearful, but had perked up somewhat with a sort of shivering pride in her own prominence. I've seen them like that before, getting the juice out of being the centre of attention even while they wish they were elsewhere. You could even say she hurried down, and she left the door of her bedroom open behind her, by the light coming through at the head of the stairs.

'Oh, Sergeant Moon!' she quavered at me from three steps up. 'Isn't it *awful*? I still can't believe it! *Can* there be some mistake? Is there any chance it *wasn't* ...?'

I said soothingly, yes, there was always a chance. And I slipped the latch of the cat basket with one hand, so that the flap fell open, and the Trinity cat was out of there and up those stairs like a black flash, startling her so much she nearly fell down the last step, and steadied herself against the wall with a small shriek. And I blurted apologies for accidentally loosing him, and went up the stairs three at a time ahead of her, before she could recover her balance.

He was up on his hind legs in her dolly little room, full of pop posters and frills and garish colours, pawing at the second drawer of her dressing table, and singing a loud, joyous, impatient song. When I came plunging in, he even looked over his shoulder at me and stood down, as though he knew I'd open the drawer for him. And I did, and he was up among her fancy undies like a shot, and digging with his front paws.

He found what he wanted just as she came in at the door. He yanked it out from among her bras and slips, and tossed it into the air, and in seconds he was on the floor with it, rolling and wrestling it, juggling it on his four paws like a circus turn, and purring fit to kill, a cat in ecstasy. A comic little thing it was, a muslin mouse with a plaited green nylon string for a tail, yellow beads for eyes, and nylon threads for whiskers, that rustled and sent out wafts of strong scent as he batted it around and sang to it. A catmint mouse, old Miss Thomson's last-minute purchase from the pet shop for her dumb friend. If you could ever call the Trinity cat dumb! The only thing she bought that day small enough to be slipped into her handbag instead of the shopping bag.

Connie let out a screech, and was across that room so fast I only just beat her to the open drawer. They were all there, the little pendant watch, the locket, the brooches, the true-lover's-knot, the purse, even the other earring. A mistake, she should have ditched both while she was about it, but she was too greedy. They were for pierced ears, anyhow, no good to Connie.

I held them out in the palm of my hand – such a large haul they made – and let her see what she'd robbed and killed for.

If she'd kept her head she might have made a fight of it even then, claimed he'd made her hide them for him, and she'd been afraid to tell on him directly, and could only think of staging that public act at church, to get him safely in custody before she came clean. But she went wild. She did the one deadly thing, turned and kicked out in a screaming fury at the Trinity cat. He was spinning like a humming top, and all she touched was the kink in his tail. He whipped round and clawed a red streak down her leg through the nylon. And then she screamed again, and began to babble through hysterical sobs that she never meant to hurt the poor old sod, that it wasn't her fault! Ever since she'd been going with young Joel she'd been seeing that little old bag going in and out, draped with her bits of gold. What in hell did an old witch like her want with jewellery? She had no *right*! At her age!

'But I never meant to hurt her! She came in too soon,' lamented Connie, still and for ever the aggrieved. 'What was I supposed to do? I had to get away, didn't I? *She was between me and the door!*'

She was half her size, too, and nearly four times her age! Ah well! What the courts would do with Connie, thank God, was none of my business. I just took her in and charged her, and got her statement. Once we had her dabs it was all over, because she'd left a bunch of them sweaty and clear on that brass candlestick. But if it hadn't been for the Trinity cat and his single-minded pursuit, scaring her into that ill-judged attempt to hand us young Joel as a scapegoat, she might, she just might, have got clean away with it. At least the boy could go home now, and count his blessings.

Not that she was very bright, of course. Who but a stupid harpy, soaked in cheap perfume and gimcrack dreams, would have hung on even to the catmint mouse, mistaking it for a herbal sachet to put among her smalls?

I saw the Trinity cat only this morning, sitting grooming in the church porch. He's getting very self-important, as if he knows he's a celebrity, though throughout he was only looking after the interests of Number One, like all cats. He's lost interest in his mouse already, now most of the scent's gone.

Ming's Biggest Prey

Patricia Highsmith

MING WAS RESTING COMFORTABLY on the foot of his mistress's bunk, when the man picked him up by the back of the neck, stuck him out on the deck and closed the cabin door. Ming's blue eyes widened in shock and brief anger, then nearly closed again because of the brilliant sunlight. It was not the first time Ming had been thrust out of the cabin rudely, and Ming realised that the man did it when his mistress, Elaine, was not looking.

The sailboat now offered no shelter from the sun, but Ming was not yet too warm. He leapt easily to the cabin roof and stepped on to the coil of rope just behind the mast. Ming liked the rope coil as a couch because he could see everything from the height, the cup shape of the rope protected him from strong breezes and also minimised the swaying and sudden changes of angle of the *White Lark*, since it was more or less the centre point. But just now the sail had been taken down because Elaine and the man had eaten lunch, and often they had a siesta afterward, during which time, Ming knew, that the man didn't like him in the cabin. Lunchtime was all right. In fact, Ming had just lunched on delicious grilled fish and a bit of lobster. Now, lying in a relaxed curve on the coil of rope, Ming opened his mouth in a great yawn, then with his slant eyes almost closed against the strong sunlight, gazed at the beige hills and the white and pink houses and hotels that circled the bay of Acapulco. Between the *White Lark* and the shore where people splashed inaudibly, the sun twinkled on the water's surface like thousands of tiny electric lights going on and off. A water-skier went by, skimming up white spray behind him. Such activity! Ming half dozed, feeling the heat of the sun sink into his fur. Ming was from New York, and he considered Acapulco a great improvement over his environment in the first weeks of his life. He remembered a sunless box with straw on the bottom, three or four other kittens in with him, and a window behind which giant forms paused for a few moments, tried to catch his attention by tapping, then passed on.

He did not remember his mother at all. One day a young woman who smelled of something pleasant came into the place and took him away – away from the ugly, frightening smell of dogs, of medicine and parrot dung. Then they went on what Ming now knew was an aeroplane. He was quite used to aeroplanes now and rather liked them. On aeroplanes he sat on Elaine's lap, or slept on her lap, and there were always titbits to eat if he was hungry.

Elaine spent much of the day in a shop in Acapulco, where dresses and slacks and bathing suits hung on all the walls. This place smelled clean and fresh, there were flowers in pots and in boxes out front, and the floor was of cool blue-and-white tile. Ming had perfect freedom to wander out into the patio behind the shop or to sleep in his basket in a corner. There was more sunlight in front of the shop, but mischievous boys often tried to grab him if he sat in front and Ming could never relax there.

Ming liked best lying in the sun with his mistress on one of the long canvas chairs on their terrace at home. What Ming did not like were the people she sometimes invited to their house, people who spent the night, people by the score who stayed up very late eating and drinking, playing the gramophone or the piano – people who separated him from Elaine. People who stepped on his toes, people who sometimes picked him up from behind before he could do anything about it, so that he had to squirm and fight to get free, people who stroked him roughly, people who closed a door somewhere, locking him in. People! Ming detested people. In all the world, he liked only Elaine. Elaine loved him and understood him.

Especially this man called Teddie Ming detested now. Teddie was around all the time lately. Ming did not like the way Teddie looked at him, when Elaine was not watching. And sometimes Teddie, when Elaine was not near, muttered something which Ming knew was a threat. Or a command to leave the room. Ming took it calmly. Dignity was to be preserved. Besides, wasn't his mistress on his side? The man was the intruder. When Elaine was watching, the man sometimes pretended a fondness for him, but Ming always moved gracefully but unmistakably in another direction.

Ming's nap was interrupted by the sound of the cabin door opening. He heard Elaine and the man laughing and talking. The big red-orange sun was near the horizon.

'Ming!' Elaine came over to him. 'Aren't you getting cooked, darling? I thought you were in!'

'So did I!' said Teddie.

Ming purred as he always did when he awakened. Elaine picked him up gently, cradled him in her arms, and took him below into the suddenly cool shade of the cabin. She was talking to the man, and not in a gentle tone. She set Ming down in front of his dish of water, and though he was not thirsty, he drank a little to please her. Ming did feel addled by the heat and he staggered a little.

Elaine took a wet towel and wiped Ming's face, his ears and his four paws. Then she laid him gently on the bunk that smelled of Elaine's perfume but also of the man whom Ming detested.

Now his mistress and the man were quarrelling, Ming could tell from the tone. Elaine was staying with Ming, sitting on the edge of the bunk. Ming at last heard the splash that meant Teddie had dived into the water. Ming hoped he stayed there, hoped he drowned, hoped he never came back. Elaine wet a bath towel in the aluminium sink, wrung it out, spread it on the bunk and lifted Ming on to it. She brought water, and now Ming was thirsty and drank. She left him to sleep again while she washed and put away the dishes. These were comfortable sounds that Ming liked to hear.

But soon there was another splash and plop, Teddie's wet feet on the deck, and Ming was awake again.

The tone of quarrelling recommenced. Elaine went up the few steps on to the deck. Ming, tense but with his chin still resting on the moist bath towel, kept his eyes on the cabin door. It was Teddie's feet that he heard descending. Ming lifted his head slightly, aware that there was no exit behind him, that he was trapped in the cabin. The man paused with a towel in his hands, staring at Ming.

Ming relaxed completely, as he might do preparatory to a yawn, and this caused his eyes to cross. Ming then let his tongue slide a little way out of his mouth. The man started to say something, looked as if he wanted to hurl the wadded towel at Ming, but he wavered, whatever he had been going to say never got out of his mouth, and he threw the towel in the sink, then bent to wash his face. It was not the first time Ming had let his tongue slide out at Teddie. Lots of people laughed when Ming did this, if they were people at a party, for instance, and Ming rather enjoyed that. But Ming sensed that Teddie took it as a hostile gesture of some kind, which was why Ming did it deliberately to Teddie, whereas among other people, it was often an accident when Ming's tongue slid out.

The quarrelling continued. Elaine made

coffee. Ming began to feel better, and went on deck again, because the sun had now set. Elaine had started the motor, and they were gliding slowly towards the shore. Ming caught the song of birds, the odd screams, like shrill phrases, of certain birds that cried only at sunset. Ming looked forward to the adobe house on the cliff that was his and his mistress's home. He knew that the reason she did not leave him at home (where he would have been more comfortable) when she went on the boat, was because she was afraid that people might trap him, even kill him. Ming understood. People had tried to grab him from almost under Elaine's eyes. Once he had been suddenly hauled away in a cloth bag, and though fighting as hard as he could, he was not sure he would have been able to get out if Elaine had not hit the boy herself and grabbed the bag from him.

Ming had intended to jump up on the cabin roof again, but after glancing at it, he decided to save his strength, so he crouched on the warm, gently sloping deck with his feet tucked in and gazed at the approaching shore. Now he could hear guitar music from the beach. The voices of his mistress and the man had come to a halt. For a few moments, the loudest sound was the chug-chug-chug of the boat's motor. Then Ming heard the man's bare feet climbing the cabin steps. Ming did not turn his head to look at him, but his ears twitched back a little, involuntarily. Ming looked at the water just the distance of a short leap in front of him and below him. Strangely, there was no sound from the man behind him. The hair on Ming's neck prickled, and Ming glanced over his right shoulder.

At that instant, the man bent forwards and rushed at Ming with his arms outspread.

Ming was on his feet at once, darting straight towards the man, which was the only direction of safety on the rail-less deck, and the man swung his left arm and cuffed Ming in the chest. Ming went flying backwards, claws scraping the deck, but his hind legs went over the edge. Ming clung with his front feet to the sleek wood which gave him little hold, while his hind legs worked to heave him up, worked at the side of the boat which sloped to Ming's disadvantage.

The man advanced to shove a foot against Ming's paws, but Elaine came up the cabin steps just then.

'What's happening? Ming!' Ming's strong hind legs were getting him on to the deck little by little. The man had knelt as if to lend a hand. Elaine had fallen on to her knees also and had Ming by the back of the neck now.

Ming relaxed, hunched on the deck. His tail was wet. 'He fell overboard!' Teddie said. 'It's true, he's groggy. Just lurched over and fell when the boat gave a dip.'

'It's the sun. Poor Ming!' Elaine held the cat against her breast and carried him into the cabin.

'Teddie – could you steer?'

The man came down into the cabin. Elaine had Ming on the bunk and was talking softly to him. Ming's heart was still beating fast. He was alert against the man at the wheel, even though Elaine was with him. Ming was aware that they had entered the little cove where they always went before getting off the boat.

Here were the friends and allies of Teddie, whom Ming detested by association, although these were merely Mexican boys. Two or three boys in shorts called 'Señor Teddie!' and offered a hand to Elaine to climb on to the dock, took the rope attached to the front of the boat, offered to carry 'Ming! – Ming!' Ming leapt on to the dock himself and crouched, waiting for Elaine, ready to dart away from any other hand that might reach for him. And there were several brown hands making a rush for him, so that Ming had to keep jumping aside. There were laughs, yelps, stomps of bare feet on wooden boards. But there was also the reassuring voice of Elaine warning them off. Ming knew she was busy carrying off the plastic satchels, locking the cabin door. Teddie with the aid of one of the Mexican boys was stretching the canvas over the cabin now. And Elaine's sandaled feet were beside Ming.

Ming followed her as she walked away. A boy took the things Elaine was carrying, then she picked Ming up.

They got into the big car without a roof that belonged to Teddie and drove up the winding road towards Elaine's and Ming's house. One of the boys was driving. Now the tone in which Elaine and Teddie were speaking was calmer, softer. The man laughed. Ming sat tensely on his mistress's lap. He could feel her concern for him in the way she stroked him and touched the back of his neck. The man reached out to put his fingers on Ming's back, and Ming gave a low growl that rose and fell and rumbled deep in his throat.

'Well, well,' said the man, pretending to be amused, and took his hand away.

Elaine's voice had stopped in the middle of something she was saying. Ming was tired and wanted nothing more than to take a nap on the big bed at home. The bed was covered with a red-and-white striped blanket of thin wool.

Hardly had Ming thought of this, when he

found himself in the cool, fragrant atmosphere of his own home, being lowered gently on to the bed with the soft woollen cover. His mistress kissed his cheek and said something with the word hungry in it. Ming understood, at any rate. He was to tell her when he was hungry.

Ming dozed and awakened at the sound of voices on the terrace a couple of yards away, past the open glass doors. Now it was dark. Ming could see one end of the table and could tell from the quality of the light that there were candles on the table. Concha, the servant who slept in the house, was clearing the table. Ming heard her voice, then the voices of Elaine and the man. Ming smelled cigar smoke. Ming jumped to the floor and sat for a moment looking out of the door towards the terrace. He yawned, then arched his back and stretched, and limbered up his muscles by digging his claws into the thick straw carpet. Then he slipped out to the right on the terrace and glided silently down the long stairway of broad stones to the garden below. The garden was like a jungle or a forest. Avocado trees and mango trees grew as high as the terrace itself, there were bougainvillea against the wall, orchids in the trees and magnolias and several camellias which Elaine had planted. Ming could hear birds twittering and stirring in their nests. Sometimes he climbed trees to get at their nests, but tonight he was not in the mood, though he was no longer tired. The voices of his mistress and the man disturbed him. His mistress was not a friend of the man's tonight, that was plain.

Concha was probably still in the kitchen, and Ming decided to go in and ask her for something to eat. Concha liked him. One maid who had not liked him had been dismissed by Elaine. Ming thought he fancied barbecued pork. That was what his mistress and the man had eaten tonight. The breeze blew fresh from the ocean, ruffling Ming's fur slightly. Ming felt completely recovered from the awful experience of nearly falling into the sea.

Now the terrace was empty of people.

Ming went left, back into the bedroom, and was at once aware of the man's presence, though there was no light on and Ming could not see him. The man was standing by the dressing table, opening a box. Again involuntarily Ming gave a low growl which rose and fell, and Ming remained frozen in the position he had been in when he first became aware of the man, his right front paw extended for the next step. Now his ears were back, he was prepared to spring in any direction, although the man had not seen him.

'Ssss-st! Damn you!' the man said in a whisper. He stamped his foot, not very hard, to make the cat go away.

Ming did not move at all. Ming heard the soft rattle of the white necklace which belonged to his mistress. The man put it into his pocket, then moved to Ming's right, out of the door that went into the big living room. Ming now heard the clink of a bottle against glass, heard liquid being poured. Ming went through the same door and turned left towards the kitchen.

Here he meowed, and was greeted by Elaine and Concha. Concha had her radio turned on to music.

'Fish? – Pork. He likes pork,' Elaine said, speaking the odd form of words which she used with Concha.

Ming, without much difficulty, conveyed his preference for pork, and got it. He fell to with a good appetite. Concha was exclaiming 'Ah-eee-ee!' as his mistress spoke with her, spoke at length. Then Concha bent to stroke him, and Ming put up with it, still looking down at his plate, until she left off and he could finish his meal. Then Elaine left the kitchen. Concha gave him some of the tinned milk, which he loved, in his now empty saucer, and Ming lapped this up. Then he rubbed himself against her bare leg by way of thanks, and went out of the kitchen, made his way cautiously into the living room en route to the bedroom. But now Elaine and the man were out on the terrace. Ming had just entered the bedroom, when he heard Elaine call:

'Ming? Where are you?'

Ming went to the terrace door and stopped and sat on the threshold.

Elaine was sitting sideways at the end of the table and the candlelight was bright on her long fair hair, on the white of her trousers. She slapped her thigh and Ming jumped on to her lap.

The man said something in a low tone, something not nice.

Elaine replied something in the same tone. But she laughed a little.

Then the telephone rang. Elaine put Ming down and went into the living room towards the telephone.

The man finished what was in his glass, muttered something at Ming, then set the glass on the table. He got up and tried to circle Ming, or to get him towards the edge of the terrace, Ming realised, and Ming also realised that the man was drunk – therefore moving slowly and a little clumsily. The terrace had a parapet about as high as the man's hips, but it was broken by grills in three places, grills with bars wide enough for Ming to pass through, though Ming never did. He merely looked through the grills sometimes. It was plain to Ming that the man wanted to drive him through one of the grills or grab him and toss him over the terrace parapet. There was nothing easier for Ming than to elude him. Then the man picked up a chair and swung it suddenly, catching Ming on the hip. That had been quick and it hurt. Ming took the nearest exit, which was down the outside steps that led to the garden.

The man started down the steps after him. Without reflecting, Ming dashed back up the few steps he had come, keeping close to the wall which was in shadow. The man hadn't seen him, Ming knew. Ming leapt to the terrace parapet, sat down and licked a paw once to recover and collect himself. His heart beat fast as if he were in the middle of a fight. And hatred ran in his veins. Hatred burned his eyes as he crouched and listened to the man uncertainly climbing the steps below him. The man came into view.

Ming tensed himself for a jump, then

jumped as hard as he could, landing with all four feet on the man's right arm near the shoulder. Ming clung to the cloth of the man's white jacket, but they were both falling. The man groaned. Ming hung on. Branches crackled. Ming could not tell up from down. Ming jumped off the man, became aware of the direction of the earth too late, and landed on his side. Almost at the same time, he heard the thud of the man hitting the ground, then of his body rolling a little way, then there was silence. Ming had to breathe fast with his mouth open until his chest stopped hurting. From the direction of the man, he could smell drink, cigar and the sharp odour that meant fear. But the man was not moving.

Ming could now see quite well. There was even a bit of moonlight. Ming headed for the steps again, had to go a long way through the bush, over stones and sand, to where the steps began. Then he glided up and arrived once more upon the terrace.

Elaine was just coming on to the terrace. 'Teddie?' she called. Then she went back into the bedroom where she turned on a lamp. She went into the kitchen. Ming followed her. Concha had left the light on, but Concha was now in her own room, where the radio played.

Elaine opened the front door. The man's car was still in the driveway, Ming saw. Now Ming's hip had begun to hurt, or now he had begun to notice it. It caused him to limp a little. Elaine noticed this, touched his back, and asked him what was the matter. Ming only purred.

'Teddie? Where are you?' Elaine called.

She took a torch and shone it down into the garden, down among the great trunks of the avocado trees, among the orchids and the lavender and pink blossoms of the bougainvilleas. Ming, safe beside her on the terrace parapet, followed the beam of the torch with his eyes and purred with content. The man was not below here, but below and to the right. Elaine went to the terrace steps and carefully, because there was no rail here, only broad steps, pointed the beam of the light downward. Ming did not bother looking. He sat on the terrace where the steps began.

'Teddie!' she said. 'Teddie!' Then she ran down the steps. Ming still did not follow her. He heard her draw in her breath. Then she cried:

'Concha!' Elaine ran back up the steps.

Concha had come out of her room. Elaine spoke to Concha. Then Concha became excited. Elaine went to the telephone and spoke for a short while, then she and Concha went down the steps together. Ming settled himself with his paws tucked under him on the terrace, which was still faintly warm from the day's sun. A car arrived. Elaine came up the steps and went and opened the front door. Ming kept out of the way on the terrace, in a shadowy corner, as three or four strange men came out on the terrace and tramped down the steps. There was a great deal of talk below, noises of feet, breaking of bushes, and then the smell of all of them mounted the steps, the smell of tobacco, sweat and the familiar smell of blood. The man's blood. Ming was pleased, as he was pleased when he killed a bird and created this smell of blood under his own teeth. This was big prey. Ming, unnoticed by any of the others, stood up to his full height as the group passed with the corpse, and inhaled the aroma of his victory with a lifted nose.

Then suddenly the house was empty. Everyone had gone, even Concha. Ming drank a little water from his bowl in the kitchen, then went to his mistress's bed, curled against the slope of the pillows, and fell fast asleep. He was awakened by the rr-rr-rr of an unfamiliar car. Then the front door opened, and he recognised the step of Elaine and then Concha. Ming stayed where he was. Elaine and Concha talked softly for a few minutes. Then Elaine came into the bedroom. The lamp was still on. Ming watched her slowly open the box on her dressing table, and into it she let fall the white necklace that made a little clatter. Then she closed the box. She began to unbutton her shirt, but before she had finished, she flung herself on the bed and stroked Ming's head, lifted his left paw and pressed it gently so that the claws came forth.

'Oh, Ming – Ming,' she said.

Ming recognised the tones of love.

Touch Not the Cat

Catherine Aird

THEY SAID, OF COURSE, that she should have had a dog. Not a great big dog that she couldn't handle at her time of life, nor one which needed long walks night and morning whatever the weather, which she obviously couldn't have managed, and certainly not the size of dog that ate a lot, things being what they were.

Or, at least, as they thought things were.

No, what the old lady could have done with, they said – afterwards, of course – was a small dog that barked. A barking dog, they thought, would have protected her in a way that a cat never could. They said – afterwards, of course – that having a dog might have saved her.

Well, someone modified this, at the very least it might have raised the alarm. That would have been something. Somebody, they said, might just have heard a dog barking in her cottage and gone to see what the trouble was. A small dog like a chihuahua, say, or a little terrier. Everyone else's small dogs always seemed to be barking when anyone came to the door. Why hadn't she had one too, just to be on the safe side? After all, Almstone was a pretty remote little village and there weren't all that many people about there after dark these days.

They all knew the answer to why she hadn't had a dog, of course. Mrs Doughty had a cat.

But a dog would have helped.

And Mr Mackenzie next door, although both very deaf and very Scottish, might have heard a dog barking. In the event – the sad event – it had been Mr Mackenzie who had found her afterwards. On account of the milk bottles not having been taken in, that was, and very upset about it, he had been.

Old Mrs Doughty hadn't had a dog not only because she had a cat but also because she had always insisted that her cat would take care of her.

'Pusskins will look after me,' the old lady had said time and again, stroking the rather bad-tempered black-and-white moggie. 'Won't you, my lovely?'

Pusskins, who never miaowed except at

mealtimes, would arch his back and allow her to rub behind his good ear. (The other had come to grief in a memorable encounter with a ginger tom in the alley on the other side of the cottage.)

It was a great-nephew, full of undesirable book learning, who had first said that Pusskins was the old lady's familiar. He'd always thought of his great-aunt as a witch anyway, probably because she didn't wash overmuch.

His mother, who hadn't quite understood his meaning, told him not to be so forward. At the time she had had high hopes of a bracket clock that had stood on the cottage mantelpiece (without going) for as long as she could remember. As she was to tell the other relations again and again, the clock had been promised ...

Familiar or not, Pusskins was therefore eyed warily while Mrs Doughty's relations consoled themselves in the way that relations will – afterwards, of course – with saying things to each other such as, 'You didn't get to her age and go on living alone without having a mind of your own,' and, 'If she didn't want a dog on account of having that mangy old cat, then that was that, wasn't it?'

That had certainly been that in the old lady's cottage when the burglar had come and gone. That is, the police were fairly sure that he had come only as a burglar. What was unfortunately undeniable was that, though he might have come only as burglar, he had indubitably left as a murderer as well.

What was equally obvious was that the cat had not been able to protect his mistress after all. The police as well as the relations knew Pusskins had done his best, of course, because not only was there the old lady's blood everywhere in the little cottage but, most interestingly, the police said, there was also blood – human blood, that wasn't hers – on Pusskins' claws as well.

It was a young detective constable from Berebury called Crosby, who manifestly hadn't enjoyed the sight of an elderly bludgeoned head, who had first turned his wayward attention to the cat and noticed some blood there. He had even managed to get a sample of it before Pusskins – a preternaturally clean member of his species, in spite of his battered appearance – could lick it off his paws.

Which the cat had promptly tried to do.

'Be careful, Crosby,' Detective Inspector CD Sloan had adjured, seeing him with the cat. 'It might turn nasty.' It was he who, for his sins, was in charge of the murder inquiry.

'Yes, sir,' the young Constable had said, promising to take every precaution, while remarking inconsequentially that Captain Hook had killed himself by scratching behind his ear with the wrong hand.

'Nature red in tooth and claw,' was what the clever great-nephew had said when he heard about it.

His mother hadn't liked that remark either.

'And when you've finished with the animal welfare side,' the senior policeman had said to Detective Constable Crosby

Catherine Aird

with some asperity, 'you can come and give me a hand over here while we establish a common entrance.'

Common entrance, Detective Constable Crosby had learned early on, was not only an entrance examination for children going to public schools but a safe route established by the police at a murder scene for all those professionals in homicide who have to approach the body, and, having their lawful business there, mustn't accidentally destroy important evidence in the process.

'And you'd better look sharp, Crosby,' said Detective Inspector Sloan. 'The photograph boys'll be here any minute now and Dr Dabbe doesn't hang about when he's at the wheel either.'

Dr Dabbe, the consultant pathologist to the Berebury Hospitals Trust, readily gave it as his considered opinion that the cause of Mrs Doughty's death was a fracture of the base of the skull brought about by the application of a blunt instrument from above and behind.

'A heavy blunt instrument,' he added after a closer examination of Mrs Doughty's head.

'Anything you can tell us about the person who used it, doctor?' asked Detective Inspector Sloan carefully. When he was a lad, the use of heavy blunt instruments as murder weapons had been thought to be an exclusively male province, but you could never tell these days.

'Anyone with the ability to lift a club hammer,' said the pathologist briefly.

Sloan just managed not to remark that that narrowed the field nicely and asked the doctor a few questions on haematology instead.

But, as Detective Inspector Sloan presently explained to the family, who, though they might have been a bit slow to visit while the old lady was alive, had assembled quickly enough when they heard that she was dead, what help was a cat's scratch on a man unless it happened to be on his face and needed explaining away?

The blood sample, the inspector

explained to them and to a slightly crest-fallen Detective Constable Crosby, would become important only if they were able to catch the man from whom it had come – and that, he had to remind them, was not necessarily going to be easy. Blood there was, and that in plenty; other clues there were not. Someone had come and robbed and killed and gone, and that was all anyone in authority could tell them at this stage.

As well as the relatives, there had also been the next-door neighbour, Mr Mackenzie, to question, comfort, inform, pacify ... and take a statement from. Detective Inspector Sloan was never entirely clear about the actual role of a police officer in these circumstances. He knew the theoretical one backwards. Members of the Criminal Investigation Department of every constabulary were there to investigate criminal occurrences, but, like a lot of life, it seldom worked out quite as simply as that. He'd long ago come to terms with the fact that a policeman had nearly as many parts to play in life as the seven ages of Shakespeare's man.

And some of them were not so easy.

What did you say to an apparently rational neighbour at a murder scene whose main concern was an archaic, not to say primitive, belief that it portended misfortune if a cat were permitted to leap over a corpse?

'I think, sir,' he said to Mr Mackenzie as kindly as he could, 'that these days that is just felt to be superstition. I can't see what further injury a cat could possibly do to a dead body already damaged almost beyond recognition.'

Sloan knew, of course, as well as everyone else, of the hundred and one uses of a dead cat, but that was something quite different.

Mr Mackenzie insisted that this fear was a real one and not just what he had the honesty to call a 'fret' on his part. 'Why, man, do ye no' realise that a watch was kept over a corp' in Scotland in the old days expressly to stop something like that happening?'

'No, sir.'

'Funny things, cats,' mused Mr Mackenzie. 'You never know what they're thinking.'

'Just so,' agreed Sloan, meticulously
making another point, 'but we don't know
for certain whether – er – the animal in
question did actually jump over the late
Mrs Doughty, do we, sir?'

All Sloan hoped was that this subject
never ever came up in Superintendent
Leeyes's presence. Ever since the superintendent had attended an evening class on
'Physics for Everyman' he had been trying
to explain something called 'Dead Cat
Bounce' to the entire constabulary.

Without success.

Pusskins, his paws now decently clean,
was present at this family and friends con-
ference. In fact, he stared at Mr Mackenzie
as balefully as Detective Inspector Sloan
would have liked to have done, but the
latter had his pension to think of.

It soon emerged that Pusskins might
have his pension to think of too.

Therefore the cat was also present at

the subsequent meeting at which his own immediate future was decided. There was a surprising amount of competition to give him a new home. This had more to do with having an eye to the future than any concern for animal rights – it not yet being known how the old lady might have provided for him. There was a very real fear in the family that Pusskins might be the residuary legatee ...

Something else that was troubling to the – by now very – extended family was whether Mrs Doughty had had money or not. (The bracket clock had been stolen but no one knew exactly what else.) Nobody else really knew what she had had in the way of assets, except perhaps now the burglar. The family, though, to be on the safe side, was taking a distinctly Morton's Fork view of her finances – she must have had money because she hadn't spent it – and, at least until the will was read, Pusskins was safe, not to say to be pampered.

In the end the old lady's niece took Pusskins home with her, her claim – as a blood relation – over that of a nephew on Mrs Doughty's late husband's side of the family being considered superior. This delicate matter was clinched by the said nephew's wife having in the past always used an allergy to cats as an excuse for not visiting the cottage at Almstone.

Once in the niece's home, Pusskins retreated to a south-facing windowsill, where he devoted his days to lying in the sun and attending to his personal hygiene in full view of the neighbours, which the old lady's niece didn't think was very nice.

The cat alternated his pose effortlessly between couchant and rampant as the fancy took him and, to the niece's despair, ate this but not that – and then that but not this. Moral ascendancy over the niece having thus been achieved, he just waited.

And waited.

He waited for exactly seventeen days.

Even when Detective Inspector Sloan and Detective Constable Crosby – and a veterinary surgeon – came to the niece's house, Pusskins only evinced a rather languid interest in their tale of a man with some rather nasty scratches on his arms and legs who had had to consult his doctor because he had an indolent ulcer on his right leg and some very enlarged and suppurating lymph nodes.

'The doctor,' reported the police inspector with a pardonable touch of drama, it being something of a professional coup, 'diagnosed that the man was suffering from *Pasturella multicida*.'

The niece exclaimed, 'Lord, bless us, and whatever is that when it's at home?' having not yet caught up with the precise dangers of salmonella poisoning as presented by the popular press and vaguely associating the two.

'Moreover,' added Crosby, the detective constable accompanying Detective Inspector Sloan, who was determined to have his say too, 'the man had the same blood profile as the blood which the cat had on its claws.'

Even then Pusskins didn't stir. But when he heard the veterinary surgeon explain that a diagnosis of *Pasturella multicida* in the man meant that the old lady's murderer must have caught 'cat-scratch fever' from this particular member of the family *felix domesticus*, Pusskins twitched his whiskers in a very satisfied way indeed.

The Hunchback Cat

Edmund Crispin

The Hunchback Cat

Edmund Crispin

'WE'RE ALL SUPERSTITIOUS,' said Fen. And from the assembled party, relaxing by the fire, rose loud cries of dissent. 'But we are, you know,' Fen persisted, 'whether we realise it or not. Let me give you a test.'

'All right,' they said. 'Do.'

'Let me tell you about the Copping case.'

'A crime,' they gloated. 'Good.'

'And if any of you,' said Fen, 'can solve it unassisted, he (or she, of course) shall be held to be without stain.

'The Copping family was an old one, and like most old families it had its traditions, the most important of these being, unfortunately, parricide.

'This didn't always take the form of actual *murder*. Sometimes it was accident, and sometimes it was neglect, and sometimes Copping parents were driven by the insufferable behaviour of their offspring to open a vein in the bath. Nonetheless, there it was. As the toll mounted with the years, the Coppings inevitably became more and more prone to brood.

'By 1948, however, there were only

two Coppings in the direct line left alive
– Clifford Copping, a widower, and his
daughter Isobel. Isobel, moreover, was
married, and consequently no longer
lived in the family mansion near Wantage.
In August of 1948, however, she and her
husband went to Wantage for a short visit.
And that was when the thing happened.

'As for me, I was making a detour
through Wantage, on my way back from
Bath to Oxford, so as to be able to have
dinner at the White Hart. And it was in the
bar of the White Hart, at shortly after six
in the evening, that I got into conversation
with Isobel's husband, Peter Doyle. He was
drinking a fair amount. And by a quarter
to eight he had reached the stage of insist-
ing that I return with him to the Copping
house for a meal.

'I didn't at all want to do that, but as
he already knew that I'd been proposing
to dine at the pub, alone, it was difficult
to refuse. So in the end I gave in, and we
set out to walk to the house by way of the
fields.

'It was a beautiful evening: I enjoyed the walk thoroughly. There was a cat, a handsome little high-stepping tortoiseshell cat, which adopted us, following us the whole way. "She seems to want to come in," I said when we arrived at the front door. And, "That's all right," said Doyle vaguely. "Isobel and my father-in-law are both fond of cats." So she did come in, and she and I were introduced to Isobel together.

'I quite liked Isobel. But it was clear from the first that relations between her and her husband were very strained. We all talked commonplaces for a while, and then Doyle suggested that as there was still a little time to use up before dinner, he should take me to meet his father-in-law, who would probably not be joining us for the meal.

'"He hasn't been too well recently," Doyle explained. "You know, broody a bit ... But he'd never forgive me if I let you go away without his meeting you."

'Well, of course I mumbled the usual things about not wanting to be a nuisance and so forth. And I can tell you, I should have been a good deal more emphatic about them if I'd known then what the inquest subsequently brought out: that for a long time now Clifford Copping had been seriously neurotic, with suicidal tendencies ... However, I didn't know, so I allowed myself to be overruled. Her father was in the top room of the tower, Isobel said. So to the tower, still accompanied by our faithful cat, Doyle and I duly went.

'It stood apart from the rest of the house, fifty feet high or more, with smooth sheer walls and narrow slits for windows; date about 1450, I should think. I expected it to be fairly ruinous inside, but surprisingly, it wasn't. On the top landing Doyle paused in front of a certain door. I was a little way behind him, still negotiating the last flight of stairs.

'"If you don't mind waiting a moment, I'll just go in and warn him that you're here,' he said – a proposal which didn't seem to me to march very well with his assurance, earlier on, that his father-in-law would never forgive him if I left without being introduced. However, of course, I agreed – whereupon he produced from his pocket a key which I'd seen Isobel give him, and proceeded to unlock (yes, definitely it *was* locked) and to half-open the door. He looked back at me then, saying in a low voice:

"'I expect you'll think it's odd, but my father-in-law does like to be locked in here from time to time, so long as it's Isobel who keeps the key: he trusts Isobel completely. Being shut in, and having these tremendously thick walls all around him – it gives him a feeling of security. Of course, locking him*self* in is what he'd really like best, but the doctor won't allow that. That's why all the bolts have been taken away."

"'Ah,' I said. And something of what I felt must have showed in my face, because Doyle added:

"'He's all right, you know ... But naturally, if you – I mean, would you rather we didn't?'

"'*Yes, I'd very much rather,*' would have been the truthful answer to that. But

Doyle's question was plainly of a piece with the Latin *Num?*: it expected a negative – and got one. So then we stopped talking, and while I waited nervously on the stair, Doyle entered the room. And found the body.

'Actually, to be just and exact about it, it was the cat which saw the body first. While we'd been talking the cat had been looking into the room, and not at all liking what was in there. You know how they arch their backs, and the hair stands up all over the spine ...? Well, after about a minute and a half, or perhaps as much as two minutes, Doyle came out again, very slow and white and shaken, and sat down on the top stair with his head in his hands. I could have asked him questions, but I didn't. I went past him into the room and saw for myself.

'There was a kitchen knife and a severed throat and an almost inconceivable mess of blood. When I'd satisfied myself that no one was hidden there (and also that not even a child could possibly have escaped through the tiny windows) I felt Copping's skin and looked at the blood and

concluded (correctly, as it turned out) that
the wretched man had been dead at least
an hour (it was then 8:24 exactly). Then
I locked the room again and gave the key
back to Doyle, and together we returned to
the house, where he telephoned the police
and a doctor while I went off on my own
and – well, you can guess what I did, can't
you?

'The rest is easily told. Copping had
last been seen alive at 6:15, by Isobel when
she locked him into the tower room; also
he'd been seen not more than five minutes
before that by two of the servants – so if
there was any question of murder, at least
it was certain that Doyle hadn't done it ...

'And fortunately there *was* some question of murder – very much so. True, there
were no prints except Copping's own on
the knife. But low down on one of the
panels of the room you could see traces of
the blood, as if a splashed skirt-hem, say,
had brushed against it ... That wasn't done
by Doyle or myself; there was no blood on
either of us, anywhere. And it wasn't done

by Copping in his death-agony – for the simple reason that between the body and the panel a considerable area of floor was innocent of blood-spots.

'All of which meant Isobel.

'Isobel who had had the key of that virtually impregnable room. Isobel who would inherit the whole of her father's estate. Isobel in whose wardrobe, hastily hidden away, the police found a stained mackintosh ...

'That's really the lot. I told the CID my story just as I've told it to you. And do you know, at the end of it, they were *still* proposing to arrest Isobel ... Sheer superstition.' Fen got to his feet. 'Well, it's been a delightful evening, but I think I'd better be getting along now ...'

The resultant howl nearly deafened him. He shook his head at them mockmournfully. 'No true rationalists? Really none? But unless you happen to be superstitious, it's simple. Doyle's wife was preparing to divorce him, you see, thereby depriving him of his chance of a share in all that lovely inheritance. He hated her bitterly for that, and in his father-in-law's death he saw a chance of revenge. It was he, of course, who planted the stained mackintosh, in the interim before the arrival of the police: I know that much because by then I'd realised what he was up to, and quite simply followed and watched him, without his being aware of it ...'

'But, Gervase, you haven't explained anything,' wailed a fair-haired girl plaintively. 'What *we* want to know is what made you suspicious of him in the first place.'

Fen laughed. 'Oh, come now. You're none of you superstitious, you've assured me of that. And not being superstitious, you ought to be aware that it's only in melodramas and ghost stories that little tortoiseshell cats react violently to the sight of corpses. In real life I'm afraid it isn't so. For a cat to get into that alarming state there has to be some much livelier stimulus. A dog was one possibility; but a dog would have made itself heard. So how about another cat? The family were fond of cats, I'd heard, so very likely they owned one. And it wouldn't have been difficult for Doyle to stuff the wretched creature through one of the little windows ... He'd noticed the blood on the panel, you see – which of course had been smeared there by the cat – and worked it out that if the cat were disposed of, that panel could be made the foundation for a murder charge.

'Naturally, he'd have buried the cat later. But while he was telephoning the police, I was out looking for the poor thing, which eventually I found in the bushes, near the foot of the tower, where it had crawled to die. A white Siamese it was: no blood on its paws, but a big splotch, acquired obviously at the very moment of Copping's death, on its flank.'

'So Copping did it himself,' said the fair-haired girl who had spoken before. 'What a sell ...' She hesitated, and then suddenly her eyes grew shrewd. 'Or *did he*? The fact that this man Doyle tried to incriminate his wife doesn't necessarily mean that she wasn't guilty, does it?'

The Hunchback Cat

'Clever girl.' Fen smiled at her. 'Actually, it wasn't until twelve weeks later that the servant the police had suborned caught Isobel burning the blood-stained frock she'd worn to kill her father ... But better late than never. And it makes a good ending, don't you think? Nice to know that these old family traditions die so hard.'

Credits